PRESENTED TO:

_____

FROM:

_____

DATE:

_____

THE COW SAID NEIGH!

A FARM STORY

BY **RORY FEEK**

Tommy
NELSON®

An Imprint of Thomas Nelson
thomasnelson.com

ILLUSTRATED BY BRUNO ROBERT

The Cow Said Neigh!

© 2018 Rory Feek

Published in Nashville, Tennessee, by Tommy Nelson. Tommy Nelson is an imprint of Thomas Nelson. Thomas Nelson is a registered trademark of HarperCollins Christian Publishing, Inc.

Published in association with Atticus Brand Partners, 611 Shenandoah Drive, Brentwood, Tennessee 37027.

Tommy Nelson titles may be purchased in bulk for educational, business, fund-raising, or sales promotional use. For information, please e-mail SpecialMarkets@ ThomasNelson.com.

ISBN-13: 978-1-4041-1638-2 (custom)

Library of Congress Cataloging-in-Publication Data

Names: Feek, Rory Lee, author. | Robert, Bruno, 1967- illustrator.
Title: The cow said neigh! : a farm story / by Rory Feek ; illustrated by Bruno Robert.
Description: Nashville : Thomas Nelson, 2018. | Summary: Illustrations and rhyming text follow a series of farm animals as each wishes it could be another, and lets out the sound of the animal it envies.
Identifiers: LCCN 2018013859 | ISBN 9781400311712 (hardcover)
Subjects: | CYAC: Stories in rhyme. | Domestic animals--Fiction. | Animal sounds--Fiction. | Humorous stories.
Classification: LCC PZ8.3.F318 Cow 2018 | DDC [E]--dc23 LC record available at https://lccn.loc.gov/2018013859

Printed in China

21 22 23 24 25 HH 10 9 8 7 6 5 4 3 2 1

Mfr: HH / Shenzhen, China / May 2021 / PO #12078446

to Indiana

There once was a cow in a barn who could see
A horse in a field who ran wild and free.
"If I were a horse, I could run free all day."
And the cow opened his mouth and let out a big . . .

The horse heard the cow, and he looked in the pond
At the duck with the bill who swam all day long.
"If I were a duck, bet they'd stay off my back."
And the horse reared back, and out came a . . .

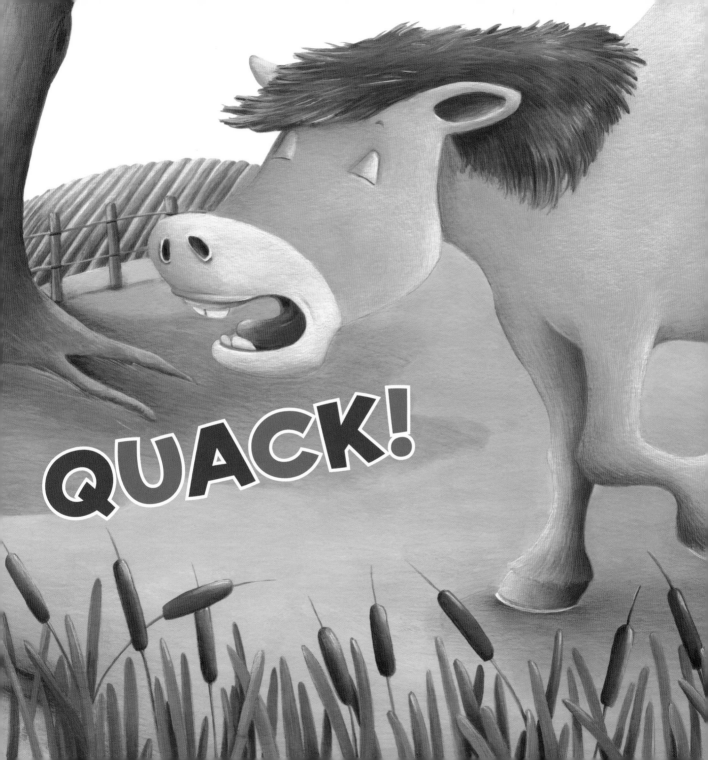

The duck heard the horse, and he saw the sheep
With a big winter coat, two inches deep.
"If I were a sheep, that would be good."
And the duck said . . .

BAA!

. . . as loud as he could.

The sheep heard the duck, and he looked at the pig
Using his nose in the deep mud to dig.
"If I were a pig, I could dig with my snout."
And the sheep opened his mouth, and an . . .

OINK!   . . . came out.

The pig heard the sheep, and he looked in the yard
At the dog on the porch who proudly stood guard.
"If I were a dog, I bet I could be tough."
And the pig wiggled his tail, and he let out a . . .

RUFF!

The dog heard the pig, and he looked in the house
At the cat on the rug that was chasing a mouse.
"If I were a cat, I'd be inside right now."
And the dog opened his mouth and let out a . . .

MEOW!

The cat heard the dog, and he left the mouse there
And looked at the farmer asleep in his chair.
"If I were a man, oh, the places I'd go."
And then the cat purred and let out a . . .

HELLO!

The farmer opened his eyes when he heard the cat,

And he thought to himself, *Did I* really *hear that?*

Then he walked to the barn, and he opened the door
And heard some more things he'd not heard before.

The cow said

NEIGH,

and
the horse
said

QUACK.

The duck said **BAA,**

and the sheep

OINKED back.

The pig said

RUFF,

and the dog said

MEOW,

As the cat and the farmer stood by the cow.

Then the farmer smiled.
What else could he do
But open his mouth and let out a big . . .

MOOOOOO!